Grandmother Cat
and
the Hermit

Grandmother Cat
and
the Hermit

Elizabeth Coatsworth

PICTURES BY IRVING BOKER

THE MACMILLAN COMPANY

For the Ranch Household,
whether humans, horses,
dogs or cats, with much love

chapter one

Grandmother Cat was an old cat. If any of the five cats had once been her child, she had long ago forgotten it. She kept herself to herself. She was very small, gray as cobwebs, with a thin tail, an uneven coat, and pale yellow eyes. She could on occasion purr but it was a very ordinary purr, and if she had ever walked about people's ankles, begging for some tidbit, she no longer bothered with such behavior. Even her mew was small and rusty with disuse.

Grandmother Cat was not a cat that anyone troubled to look at twice. She moved like a small independent shadow about the big open rooms of the house. She disappeared down the gully among the cactuses and bushes. She ate at the cat dish when she was hungry. She lapped milk when she could get it, or drank from the little pool at the end of the hose if the milk dish was empty.

None of the four children was ever unkind to her. They liked animals: horses, dogs, cats, even the bantams raising their chicks with one eye out for the coyotes which came down from the hills with the full moon. No one was kind or unkind to Grandmother Cat except Dave. And it was not so much that he had chosen her for a companion as that she had chosen him.

Dave was the second of the children. He had an older sister interested now in teen-age affairs, a younger sister always reading, and a little brother too small to be of much practical use.

Somehow Dave, like Grandmother Cat, was often busy with his own affairs. But he was not alone. Wherever he went Grandmother Cat went, too, a small homely little figure. She understood about school, at least that she could walk only as far as the school bus that waited every morning in the grove of live oaks at the foot of their drive.

When Dave came home she was somewhere around.

"Hi! Grandmother Cat!" he might say when he saw her. Or he might say nothing.

When he went up to the corral to feed and water the three horses, she went along with him, usually out of sight. If he rode his bicycle round and round the island of wild growth circled by the drive, she lay in the shade and watched him. If his mother read aloud to the four children in her room, Grandmother Cat was under the bed. The big dogs might give her a poke with the tip of a nose as they went by. Grandmother Cat was neither pleased nor displeased by the attention.

But when bedtime came, she was on hand to jump on Dave's bed and curl up in a small gray muff at his knees. And there she slept all night, leaving night hunting to younger cats.

Their best times were when Dave went exploring on foot, and Grandmother Cat went along. Elizabeth had

teen-age friends she wanted to see. Jenny was up in the oak tree house with a book. As for Tom, he was here, there, and everywhere. Anyone could trace him by his laughter, his shouts, or by the trail of odds and ends left behind. He was too little and too noisy to go for long, hard walks in the hills. In ten minutes he would be saying, "Let's eat our lunch now," or "Let's go home, Dave. My feet hurt."

Only Dave and Grandmother Cat liked to explore. On all sides between their place and the high mountains lay the foothills in a tumble of ridges and arroyos, fire-breaks, old trails, shallow streams, forgotten falls, hidden groves of trees, and, once in a great while, in the lower hills, the ruin of some small building, perhaps once an old Spanish ranch house, or perhaps a prospector's shanty.

One Saturday morning after the spring rains, Dave put up a lunch, including a slice of meat for Grandmother Cat, spoke to his mother, who was going riding with the two girls, and started off.

He didn't have to call Grandmother Cat. She was there under a manzanita bush, apparently thinking about something else.

"Well, off we go, Grandmother," said Dave.

"Prrp," answered Grandmother Cat.

They had never explored very far to the west of

4

their own ridge, but from the firebreak above it, Dave had once seen a far-off arroyo with live-oak trees dark along its sides, sheltered from the wind.

"We're going a long way today, Grandmother Cat," warned Dave. "Think you can make it?"

Grandmother Cat stared at him. "Any place you can go, I can go," she seemed to be saying. "After all, I may be old but I am still a cat."

So off they went westward across country over ridges and down into gullies and arroyos, along deer trails, and through rough prickly brush that scratched Dave's bare arms and legs and snapped back into his face, while the cat moved more easily, close to the ground, a very little ahead of Dave.

Once she froze, and her stillness gave Dave warning, so that he, too, stood still while a rattlesnake slowly coiled its way across their path and disappeared again among low-growing bushes.

Undisturbed, Dave and Grandmother Cat kept climbing wherever they could, getting higher and higher above the valley. Several times Dave caught sight of the arroyo he was heading for, but it was even farther off than he had thought.

"Let's have lunch," he said to Grandmother Cat, and they sat side by side in the shade of a bush, he eating sandwiches while she had her slice of meat, and the

6

last of the milk in the cup of the Thermos bottle when Dave had finished the rest.

Suddenly she stopped lapping and listened, motionless for a long time. Then she returned to her drinking as if nothing had happened.

"Was it a mountain lion?" Dave asked her. "Or only a deer?" He had seen deer several times, but never a mountain lion, though once he had seen their tracks in the soft earth near a stream.

A little chill went down Dave's spine at the thought that a mountain lion might have been watching them and then slipped away. He was not really afraid. It was part of the wonder of the hills that many creatures lived there in secret, and many eyes spied on their passing.

Dave put the sandwich wrappings and the empty Thermos bottle back into his knapsack.

"All right, Grandmother Cat?" he asked. "All through? Then, on to the canyon!"

chapter two

It was almost mid-afternoon when Dave and Grandmother Cat came to the firebreak that overlooked
the canyon. The place was so beautiful that Dave just
sat down to look at it for a while, and Grandmother Cat
lay in the shade and closed her eyes. Beauty as such
meant nothing to her.

But to Dave it did and this canyon was the most beautiful place he had ever seen. Just below him it widened a
little and here half a dozen big sycamore trees grew
beside a slow-running stream. They were old trees,
with pale spotted bark, and Dave knew that their pres-
ence showed that the stream ran all year round, not

just after the rains as so many did. What's more there was sand along each bank, and he could see a number of tracks marking it, where the mountain creatures came to drink.

The sides of the canyon were beautiful, too, with the lavender of wild lilac and the creamy white small blossoms of buckbrush. The yucca candles were in bud, rising high from their candlesticks of sharp leaves, and there were patches of low flowers to which, like Grandmother Cat, he paid no attention except to be glad that they were there.

"We can't sit here all day!" he exclaimed, having rested for a few minutes and got a general view of this part of the canyon. "Come on, Grandma! Get a-going!"

Grandmother Cat glanced at him to remind him that stopping had not been her idea in the first place, and then they made their steep rough way down into the arroyo. There was no trail. Sometimes Dave jumped from rock to rock, more often he slid; but Grandmother Cat was a better mountaineer than he was. The little gray pegs of her feet found a hold everywhere, and although she occasionally jumped, she never slid. She wisely kept a little to one side of his descent, so as to avoid the sliding pebbles and loose dirt that marked his path.

Side by side they arrived at the bottom of the canyon

and side by side they stooped to drink of the clear murmurous water.

Then they both raised their heads and looked around them. Each glanced at the sycamores to see if they were easy to climb and Dave noticed a big round of mistletoe growing like an orchid on one branch, which he thought he could reach if he should come back here a little before Christmas.

But having glanced at the trees, Dave and Grandmother Cat studied the prints in the sand. There were many arrow-shaped ones left by the hoofs of deer. It was Grandmother Cat who, with her lip pulled back a little to show the tips of her longer teeth, sniffed at the tracks of coyotes, and so pointed them out to Dave. The pad prints had not been made recently. The sand at the edges was crumbling and they were more important to Grandmother Cat than to Dave.

"They haven't been here for a week," he told her. "Anyway, I'll take care of you. Coyotes are afraid of human beings, even of boys."

It was then that he saw the other track, the one that looked like a bear's, and yet different. It was large and flat with the print of toes but not of claws, and instead of coming to the stream and going away again after drinking like the other tracks, it followed along the edge of the water, headed up canyon.

"I don't like the looks of it," said Dave, in a low

10

voice. "There *are* bears in these mountains. Why, there's even a lake called Big Bear Lake not thirty miles from here. I've never seen a bear track and this doesn't look just the way I thought one would, but I

guess it must be a bear, and I don't think it was here very long ago."

He had to lift Grandmother Cat up and put her right on one of the footprints before she would sniff at it and then she didn't seem much interested.

"Maybe cats don't know about bears," Dave reflected. "Grandmother Cat," he told her, "I don't think your mother brought you up right. Bears are a great deal more dangerous than coyotes. We'd better go back."

"Yes, you certainly ought to go back," said Dave's conscience sharply. "You're going to be late for supper as it is. You may get lost going home."

But now, Dave began to argue with his conscience. "No one will mind my being late. They understand about how easy it is to get lost in the hills. I can have something in the kitchen."

His conscience made one last effort. "You're not lost," it said. "At least not now, though you may be later. You're just pigheaded. And that track *is* funny. You ought to stay away from things you don't understand."

"Then how will I ever get to understand anything new?" Dave argued back. "I'm not following the track. I'm just seeing what the canyon looks like a little higher up."

"Don't take long," said his conscience weakly. Perhaps it, too, wondered what lay behind the next curve of the stream.

While Dave and his conscience, or maybe it was his caution, argued, Grandmother lay quietly resting. She might almost have been listening to Dave's thoughts, for at this minute she rose and trotted up stream with Dave following.

The next curve of the stream was not so beautiful. There was only one sycamore and more stones and less sand along the banks. But even here it pleased Dave. A canyon wren was singing and another answered it from a ridge. A trickle of water came down the steep west slope and in one place flowed through an up-tilted wild meadow, very green, and no larger than the big room in his own house. It was criss-crossed by tracks.

"The deer come here, Grandmother Cat," Dave said aloud.

But more than deer came there. Watching the bank of the stream he saw two very large old paw prints where a mountain lion had crouched on a rock and set its front feet in the sand while it drank.

Mountain lions were rare in the hills. Dave knew no one who had ever really seen one, but his father had told him that they weren't dangerous to men. Would the great cat know that Dave *was* a man? He began to whistle to let any mountain lion which might be around know that he was there.

This time Grandmother Cat crouched as she sniffed the tracks, and all her rough hair rose along her back until she looked twice her usual size. Her pale yellow eyes glared and she walked away from the spot stiff-legged and on her guard.

"It's all right, Grandmother Cat," said Dave. "He was here days ago. You're safe. And you're with me."

Dave always spoke quietly to animals, and moved quietly when he was near them. In return, they trusted him. Now at the sound of his voice, Grandmother Cat relaxed and went on at her natural gait, only looking over her shoulder now and then at the hillside above them with all its little paths almost hidden under wild lilac and buckbrush, sage, and manzanita with its blood-red bark.

There were no more sycamores beyond the next bend. The canyon was too narrow and sunless for them to grow here. Instead live oaks began to appear in the crevices of the slopes, a few of them big trees with wide-spreading branches. The stream ran over stones and sang against boulders. Dave could see no sign of any tracks except the very occasional, never quite clear print of what he took to be a bear.

"You're not afraid of a bear, are you, Grandmother Cat?" asked Dave, leaning down to stroke her back, and she looked up and said, "Prrp," in return, a sound she made for no one else but Dave and not often for him.

"I'm not afraid, either," said Dave.

But he was lying.

14

chapter three

Unexpectedly, and suddenly, they had come to the head of the canyon, or rather to its two heads, for like the old heraldic eagles, the canyon was double-headed.

On the east it ended in a great amphitheater of tumbled rock as if the whole cliff had broken off. The stone was almost rose colored in the afternoon light, and this branch of the stream bed was so filled with boulders that there was scarcely room for the water to force its way, scolding, through them. There was no sign of a waterfall. There must be springs at the head of the arroyo which fed this small flow of living water.

15

The top of the cliff overhung the bottom. Nothing could climb such a place. It was beautiful, barren, and fierce.

The western horn of the canyon was altogether different. The place was green with ferns and live-oak trees and a narrow waterfall shone white from the high slope at its end.

Between these two canyons lay a triangle of land, like a ship of earth and rock. It seemed to be flat on top. On the rocky canyon side the bank of this promontory also appeared unclimbable, the top overhanging as it did in the rest of the canyon. In the western canyon, too, the banks were very steep but here there grew the oaks that Dave had seen from the distance.

This earth ship was backed by a perpendicular cliff. It was perfectly smooth, and towered up, colored rose like the rest of the rock face except for a dark stain that ran roughly down its center.

In all his explorations Dave had never come upon such a place as this. The eastern canyon filled him with awe, the western canyon with delight, and the ship-shaped flats between them with curiosity.

But something cautioned Dave not to be too much in a hurry. He crouched behind a large manzanita bush and took Grandmother Cat in his arms, for she seemed anxious to follow on into the western canyon.

16

"Wait," he whispered to her. "There's something strange here. We want to see where we're going."

She gave a rusty, impatient mew.

"Those queer tracks go right on," whispered Dave. "I still don't like the look of them. Suppose a bear has his den up in here?"

Grandmother Cat struggled suddenly to get out of Dave's arms and then apparently giving up the attempt, relaxed and purred a little.

There was something here, something different, but the boy couldn't put his finger on it. There seemed no life anywhere except for the canyon wrens singing on every side, mingling their short sweet songs with the sounds of running water. Nothing living moved on the hillside among the ferns, nothing moved along the two streams as they flowed down their separate canyons to meet at the prow of the projecting flats between them.

"I wonder what's up there," thought Dave. "Could a bear have his den there?"

He looked for a path up the greener slope, which he thought he could climb if he tried.

As he was making up his mind what to do, Dave's eye was caught by a vague motion against the flat rock at the back of the flats.

"It must be spray," he decided. "There must be a small waterfall behind it. It moves with the wind."

At the far end of the green slope, which he had been considering climbing, there was a tumble of rocks. At first Dave scarcely noticed it among all the other things to be seen, but suddenly he caught a glimpse of some movement behind one of the boulders.

Grandmother Cat gave a wriggle, slipped out of Dave's arms, and started off toward the motion, holding her tail straight in the air as she did when she was pleased.

"Grandmother! Grandmother! Here, kitty! kitty!" Dave called softly, but Grandmother Cat, usually so quick to come when he called, this time paid no attention, but walked on, head and tail held high.

Dave got to his feet to follow her and just as he appeared out of the shadow of the manzanita, a voice which seemed to boom from all the canyon walls called,

"Who's there?" And from behind the rocks, halfway down the slide, came a strange figure.

"At least, it isn't a bear," thought Dave with relief, though the voice had reverberated almost like a bear's growl.

Dave stood still, motionless with surprise.

The man who had arrived so suddenly was bearded with hair as gray and rough as Grandmother Cat's own fur. Over his shoulders hung a wooden yoke from which dangled two empty pails. He stood at ease, staring from under shaggy brows in silence at the boy and the cat.

"Your cat isn't afraid of me," said the man at last. "You've no cause to be, either."

"I'm not," said Dave and then added uneasily, "I'm not afraid of anyone on earth."

"That's a pretty bold statement," said the stranger. "Then you won't mind coming up to have a talk? You can carry one of the pails of water if you've a mind to."

And he disappeared out of sight behind the tumble of rocks, only to appear a few minutes later by the pool at the bottom of the falls.

Grandmother Cat ran to him at once and rubbed herself against his ankles, a thing she never did to anyone except once in a great while, to Dave. The man reached down and stroked her and when he stopped, Grandmother Cat raised herself on her hind legs to push her round hard head into the palm of his withdrawing hand.

"She doesn't usually like people," said Dave.

"Animals know their friends," said the man, smiling. "My friends are all animals—with two exceptions."

Paying no further attention to Dave, the man leaned over and filled the empty tin pails with water. Then straightening, he picked up one in his hand and said to Dave,

"Are you strong enough to carry the other up the trail?"

"Sure," said Dave.

The man smiled.

"It's not easy," he said, leading the way. "Not easy even for me."

It was not easy. Following carefully, Dave discovered that hidden behind a natural wall of boulders there was a staircase of sorts up the steep slope, some of it natural, and some of it made by fitting in flat-topped or slanting rocks between the boulders of the slide. The steps were uneven, some very short, and some high, so that Dave often had to set the pail above him and scramble up after it. Some of the stones moved under his feet, but the man ahead of him climbed with the assurance of long familiarity, knowing just where to set each foot in exactly the right spot.

It was these feet, almost on the level with his eyes, at which Dave now stared. They wore cowhide sandals, tied with thongs above the ankles and over the insteps, but only reaching to the base of the toes, leaving the toes themselves free to grip the rocks they stepped on, almost like fingers.

"The bear's track!" thought Dave, and as if he had read his thoughts, the man above him looked down and said, smiling,

"I saw you studying my footprints as you came along. Bet you, you thought they were a bear's. Yes, a bear's."

"Bet you I did," said Dave, grinning.

"But the cat knew better," said the man. "Cats always do—all animals do. I'm not a bear, you can see for yourself. I'm only a hermit. Only a hermit."

chapter four

At the top of the climb, the land was almost perfectly flat. Close to the cliff with its stain stood a low building made of boulders chinked with moss and roofed with branches and overlapping bunches of grass. Part of the building was underground. The moving something which Dave had noticed along the face of the cliff was not water but a thin, almost imperceptible column of smoke. Close to the hut, a vegetable garden was neatly planted.

The hermit emptied some of the water in his pail into a stone with a round hollow in it.

"That is a metate, the kind Indian women used for grinding their corn into meal," he said. "I found it right here. Now the quail and rabbits like to drink from it when they come visiting. They have plenty of water in the stream but this is safer. An animal or bird is never so helpless as when it stoops to drink. Then it is really helpless."

There was an unplanted space in front of the heavy wooden door, and here the hermit brought out two homemade chairs.

"Sit you down, sit you down," he said. "You'll want to look about you before we go into the cabin. Look about you all you want."

Dave noticed that the hermit was likely to repeat a phrase twice and sometimes three times, and guessed that it came from his seldom having anyone but the animals to talk to.

Now the hermit sat back, his brown eyes under the thatch of gray eyebrows looking about him with pleasure.

"That fenced-in part covering most of my land is barley. At first I had a hard time, yes, a hard time keeping the deer out of that patch. But they want to please me. They're anxious to. Now they keep out of it. The vegetables, too. Oh, once in a while a lettuce or a cabbage will be nibbled. But not often. The rabbits are more obstinate than the deer. Yes, a rabbit is obstinate, and I have to keep an eye out for the burro. Yes, I have to keep my eye on that fellow all the time he's here."

While he was speaking two quail with long plumes above their dark headdresses slipped out from the garden and went to the water to drink. A wren joined

them, bending forward to take a few sips. Then a wild rabbit hopped into the circle.

Dave reached quietly forward to pick up Grandmother Cat, but the hermit said in his usual voice,

"Let her be, let her be. She understands that you're all guests here."

Even when the old coyote climbed the steps and came up to the hermit for the piece of barley bread he had in the pouch at his belt, Grandmother Cat only ruffled her tail and flattened low for a minute.

"Oh, come here, cat," called the hermit a little impatiently. "Cat, come, come, come."

And Grandmother Cat came, walking on tiptoe. The coyote stared at her for a moment and then wagged the tip of his brush. The hermit laid his hands lightly on both their backs. Stroking and talking softly to them he brought the two animals nearer and nearer together.

"He'll pounce!" cried Dave in a low voice. "Don't! She can't protect herself."

Grandmother Cat and the coyote both stiffened at Dave's voice, and the hermit glanced at him with a frown.

"Keep still boy!" he said softly. "Keep still!"

And he went on patting and talking to the two animals until the coyote reached down his muzzle and touched Grandmother Cat's.

A moment later, Grandmother Cat was twining about the coyote's legs, giving her small uneven purr.

"They're friends now," said the man, looking again

at Dave. "Forget about them altogether. Forget about them."

Now Dave was looking at the hermit, and for the first time he seemed like an old man.

"How tired you look!" he exclaimed, suddenly troubled.

"It will pass. It will pass," said the hermit. "For a little while one gives oneself, all of oneself. That is the only way to keep the Peaceable Kingdom."

The coyote did not stay long. He came up to the hermit again to have his head rubbed, gave Dave a questioning but friendly look, nudged Grandmother Cat in the side as he went by—she flicked at him with her paw —took another lap of water, pushing the rabbit to one side, and then disappeared down the boulder staircase into the canyon below.

"A short visit," said the hermit. "Sometimes he will sleep for an hour or two in the sun. But he has to get used to you. He saw that you were nervous. He must get used to you and you to him. He has accepted the cat."

"Her name is Grandmother Cat," said Dave.

"Yes, of course, Grandmother Cat. Grandmother Cat, of course."

Grandmother Cat jumped into the hermit's lap,

28

turned once around and lay down. Dave felt a little pang of jealousy. As before, the old man seemed to read his thoughts.

"Here all love is shared," he said quietly. "Shared."

"May I pat the rabbit?"

"Of course," said the hermit. "Here's a crust to give her. When you walk up to her, keep in mind that she will not be afraid."

The rabbit was not afraid. She let Dave feed her and scratch her behind the ears. He even stroked the quail and fed them a few crumbs. When he went back to his chair the hermit's eyes were closed and he seemed asleep. As Dave sat down, the hermit woke, smiling. The tired look was gone from his face. He seemed much younger now.

"You can learn much from a cat, boy," he remarked. "All animals take naps to restore themselves or pass the time. But perhaps cats do it most. Yes, they do it most. Even people have noticed. Even people speak about taking a cat nap."

"You look much better," said Dave. He knew he shouldn't make personal remarks to grownups, but with the hermit he could say what he thought and the hermit would understand.

"Thank you, boy," said the hermit, smiling.

"My name is Dave," said Dave, a little shyly. He didn't mind being called "boy," but Dave seemed to fit him better.

"Thank you, Dave," said the hermit. "Do you see what's in my garden? Those are beets, and next to them are carrots, then onions, and peas and a few beans. Right by the cabin are two rows of corn. I can't water the barley. It grows during the rains and then withers, but I get enough to grind in the metate for most of my bread. The vegetables I do water after the rains are over. It's hard work lugging up the pails. I raise that garden by the sweat of my brow, yes, by the sweat of my brow."

Dave had a mechanical turn of mind.

"Couldn't you rig up a pipe near the top of the waterfall, maybe with some sort of funnel, and bring a flow of water down to the flats?" he asked.

The hermit slapped his knee. "Never thought of it!" he exclaimed. "I certainly haven't the sense I was born with, have I?" He laughed a rumbling laugh. "It took Dave here just a minute to figure it out and I've been lugging water for years."

Dave couldn't remember when he had felt so pleased.

"Do you know where you can get the pipe and funnel and something to hold them in place?"

30

"Yes, I know that, Dave. I know where I can get them."

"The rabbit is nibbling one of your lettuces," Dave exclaimed.

"Scoot! You little rascal!" cried the hermit. The rabbit looked up, took another nibble, and disappeared down the staircase.

"Maybe you and Grandmother Cat would like to see the house, Dave," said the hermit. "There's nothing with more curiosity than a cat, unless it's a boy."

chapter five

The door of the cabin was so low that even Dave had to stoop to enter when the hermit pulled it open. Grandmother Cat waited for no invitation. In she slipped like a shadow and began exploring before Dave's eyes were used to the dusk. The roof was higher than he had supposed, at least a foot above the hermit's head, standing.

"You see, boy," the hermit explained, "whoever built this hideaway made it so it can't be seen from the arroyo. The paving of this floor is nearly three feet underground. The fireplace is the best I've ever seen, shallow, built against the solid cliff. If you use dry wood there's almost no smoke."

The place looked like a cave but a comfortable cave. The two chairs were still outside but there was a homemade table, sandpapered smooth, with an old-fashioned oil lamp on one side.

On the floor to one side was a mattress stuffed with dry ferns, as the hermit told Dave, with two heavy blankets spread over it. On the other side of the room was a chest with the word "Hermit" printed across the top in brass-headed nails.

The hermit looked at it with a little embarrassment.

"I made that when I first came here," he explained. "I was kind of boasting, wasn't I?"

"But you *are* a hermit!" Dave had never dreamed of knowing a hermit, and he was proud of this one.

"In a manner of speaking, in a manner of speaking," said the man and turned the subject. "See those windows? They were the hardest thing I had to do when I settled in. I didn't build this house, of course. I'm just here by squatter's rights. It was built by someone a long time ago as a hideaway, I should think. He didn't have any windows in it. Just four small openings he could shoot out of, like a fort."

"Who do you think he was?" asked Dave, openmouthed.

"I don't know. He left nothing behind him but what's hanging in the corner over there."

Dave went to the place and found a frayed halter hanging on a rusty nail.

"Is that horsehair?" he asked, when he had touched it carefully, for it was very brittle.

"Yes, braided," said the hermit. "He must have had a horse, but my guess is that he kept it in another canyon. If strange horses should come up the stream, any horse will whinny. Besides, it would be hard to keep a horse where it couldn't be seen."

Dave was fascinated. He stood in the middle of the room frowning.

"Wouldn't this be a sort of trap as well as a fort?" he asked. "There's only one way up to it, isn't there?"

"Most forts are traps," the hermit said. "But our man had thought that out. Come outside for a minute."

Some distance from the cabin a narrow seam of darker rock led up the face of the cliff. In this had been chiseled a series of small notches, leading up to the faraway top.

"Hand holds and toe holds," said the hermit.

Dave at once pulled off his sneakers and started to climb.

"No! Come back," said the hermit. "Come back, I

said! A man in danger could climb up those when they were new, but rain and frost have done their work. When I first came here, I climbed them once out of curiosity, but never again. And don't you, either. It's too risky."

"All right," said Dave, a little sulkily.

When they got back to the cabin, Grandmother Cat was curled up for a nap in the middle of the hermit's bed.

"A sensible cat, Grandmother," said the hermit approvingly. "Now let's see. Here's my grocery shop." He pointed to a shelf on which were arranged the necessities: salt, pepper, lard, sugar, flour, ground barley, and tea.

"I like tea better than coffee," said the hermit. "Of course I can get along without it, and often do."

"But haven't you any eggs or meat or anything?"

"Eggs I sometimes have, but not meat. That's why I get along so well with the deer. They can smell a meat-eater and he scares them. Remember, the vegtables outside usually get ripe one at a time. They're the mainstay of my diet."

"But in winter?" asked Dave. Unconsciously he had begun to repeat himself like the hermit. "What do you eat in winter?"

"Oh, winter," said the hermit vaguely. "Winter is another story again."

Dave had come upon a second shelf, a very small one this time. On it were two books, a Bible and the collected plays of William Shakespeare.

He glanced at them.

"I can bring you books," he said eagerly. "At home we have scads and scads of them."

The hermit gave him a warm smile. "Bless you," he said. "They'd only clutter my mind. There is more in those two books than I can ponder in my lifetime. Abe Lincoln read them and reread them, and so do I."

There seemed nothing more to see and Dave's mind went back to the windows. "Did you carry them up the steps?" he asked.

"Yes," said the hermit. "Let's go outside and sit while I tell you. This late afternoon and dawn are the best times of the day. The windows had to be small, for a window is heavy, and my front steps are steep, as you know. I broke one window bringing it up and had to get another. They came from an empty half-ruined house back from the highway. I had a hard time finding three windows with all their panes still in."

He sat for a while watching the light catch the wild lilac bushes that along with the live oaks clothed the opposite hillside of the western canyon which the her-

38

mit said was named Fern. The other short branch was Cliff Canyon. Dave nodded. He liked to know the names of things. Then the hermit went on.

"When I got the windows up, I had to tear down a lot of the wall of the cabin to fit them in. *And* build it up again. It wasn't easy, but of course the stones were all there. I didn't have to bring them up as the other fellow had brought them, after building the stair. Oh yes, he built the stair. It took me a long time to find it since it needed mending, too."

A thought had been troubling Dave and now he voiced it. Somehow he felt that he could ask the hermit anything.

"No one's after you, are they?" he asked uneasily.

For the first time since Dave had met him, the hermit threw back his head and laughed.

"If you mean the sheriff, boy, no, he isn't after me. But the whole world is. Too much noise, too much dashing about after nothing, too many things that aren't needed, too many houses, too many people, too much of everything. You've heard what the psalmist said, 'I will lift up mine eyes unto the hills from whence cometh my help'? Well, I've lifted up my whole self unto the hills, where I can live and think in peace."

"Maybe I will, too," said Dave. "Grandmother Cat and I like being in the hills all day."

But the hermit shook his head.

"I don't advise it, boy," he said. "There are things for it, and things against it as I realize more and more. For a boy with a family it's not the best way. Go along as you're going now, and come to see me again. Let's say when the yucca is in bloom. You're the only human visitor except one I've ever had and now I've talked myself out for the next few weeks. But you and Grandmother Cat must be sure to come again when the yucca's in bloom. Now I'll tell you a much quicker way to get home than the way you came."

"But how do you know where I live?" asked Dave, staring. "I haven't told you."

"A hermit knows a lot more about his neighbors than his neighbors know about him," the man said, smiling. "I've watched you and Grandmother Cat often and liked what I saw of you both. Now remember, word of honor, all this is a secret. From everybody. Like a dream of the night you don't talk about in the morning."

chapter six

It was hard to wait, but Dave and Grandmother Cat waited until the first yucca was in bloom on the foothill just behind their house. It was like a tall white candle, taller than Dave.

He waited until he could see three. He didn't want to crowd things. He wanted to make sure that the hermit's yuccas were in bloom, too, and that he would be expecting them.

This time they started early in the morning. School was out so Dave chose a cool morning in the middle of the week. While he was making his sandwiches and filling the small Thermos bottle, his mother passed by the

door and said, "We're going riding later. You can ride double with Tom. But perhaps you'd rather go exploring with Grandmother Cat."

"Yes, if you don't mind," said Dave.

And then all of a sudden Tom wanted to tag along. He teased to come, but Dave stood his ground.

"Maybe you can come next time I go for the day, if you stop bothering me now," he half promised. Sometime he'd take Tom up to Johnson's Flats where they were almost certain to see deer. But he couldn't take him to visit the hermit, even if he wanted to. And he didn't. The hermit was his friend, his and Grandmother Cat's.

"We need a new horse for this family," said Mother, pausing in the kitchen on her way to make beds. "I'm going to ask Daddy if he won't give me one for my birthday. On every trip, Pompey's an unwilling goer all the way out. He'll come back fast enough. But I want a horse as fiery and gentle as—"

She paused, and Dave finished her sentence instantly.

"As a unicorn," he said.

"Yes!" exclaimed his mother. "As a unicorn. That's it exactly."

Elizabeth's voice floated in from her bedroom which she was tidying.

"Unicorns are mythical, Mother."

"Nonsense!" retorted her mother with spirit. "You just have never happened to see one," and she wandered off.

"A hermit is almost as unusual as a unicorn," Dave told Grandmother Cat as they started for the canyon,

43

taking the short way that the hermit had taught him which made use of the farm roads and connecting paths that ran along at the foot of the hills behind the valley's groves and ranches, like different sorts of string knotted together. In this lower land the mockingbirds were singing and some of the lemon trees were in bloom. At Mr. Dunhill's place they loitered to watch the horses in the pasture. Mr. Dunhill raised horses, bought horses, and sometimes sold them. Dave's mother often stopped the car on the black-top road on the outer side of the pasture to see what horses were grazing there, just as Dave and Grandmother Cat were stopping now. Dave was his mother's child in that way. Daddy could take horses or leave them. There were other things he cared for more, and two of the four children were like him. Only Dave and Jenny had their mother's eye for a horse.

Now Dave found himself watching a blue gelding, a big horse and new, for he grazed by himself. Everything he did he did strongly. His step was springy. He ate vigorously. When he raised his head to look at something, he raised it high and suddenly. Once he looked at Dave and Grandmother Cat and his eyes were unusually large. Dave felt the glance like a sound, or a touch. It wasn't fierce or sullen. It was masterful and inquiring.

It was for the sake of the pasture that Mr. Dunhill had dammed the end of Fern Canyon, making it impassable from the valley. There he had a reservoir to keep his grass irrigated all year and his horses could graze even in the dry months when the rain never fell and other people's pastures turned parched and almost useless.

"That dam is my locked gate," the hermit had said when he gave Dave directions for going home. "It closes off Fern Canyon so that no one is tempted to see what's in it. You have to leave Fern Canyon and climb the steep ridge to the west and go out and come in by little Dry Canyon. And remember, always use a different route so that you won't leave any marked trail."

That was what Dave and Grandmother Cat did now. She knew where they were going. She used the same trail she had used a month earlier, but a cat's trail doesn't matter. Dave was careful to go a little deeper into Dry Canyon and climb up by a different way.

When they came to the diminished stream whispering with summer softness among its boulders, Dave had a sense of having come home. Fern Canyon below the forks was if anything more beautiful than when they had first come upon it. After they had eaten their lunch on a rock by the sycamores, during which Dave sat with his feet in the water, they came to a stretch where all the bank was yellow with tall wild lilies. Each stem carried eight or even twelve flowers, hanging like big freckled bells, four to a tier. Dave had seen pictures of Chinese pagodas, with bells hanging from each roof, and he called these the pagoda lilies.

He had seen them before, when he was riding, but only three or four together. Here there were dozens of them and the tinkling sound of the water over the pebbles was like the sound that the flowers might make in the wind. The wild lilac and creamy buckbrush were no longer in bloom. Instead the first yuccas lifted their tall stems, thick set with white bells. But the yucca bells were closed. They would not ring as the lillies seemed to. Their magic was different.

Slowly Dave walked on and Grandmother Cat this time followed at his heels, as if she understood that for a time Dave wanted to be all alone.

When they had passed the lilies, she took her usual position, a little ahead of Dave. He sometimes wondered if she weren't trying to take care of him, to look out for snakes or for dangerous animals, with her keener animal senses.

But in the twin canyons there was no danger. High above them at the edge of the flats, the hermit was standing as if waiting for them like the lookout on a great ship.

"Hi, David! Hi, Grandmother Cat! Glad to see you!" he shouted.

"Did you know we were coming?" Dave called back.

"Of course," said the hermit. "Everyone knew. The pair of doves told me, and the quail and the doe with her fawn. I couldn't persuade her to stay, but perhaps she'll come back. No water to carry today. You see I followed your suggestion."

And looking up at the falls, Dave saw that a system had been rigged to take a share of the water to the flats. That had been *his* idea. It was lucky he had come to see the hermit or that Grandmother Cat had brought him.

"We'll be up in a jiffy," he called and at the muffled pride in his voice Grandmother Cat turned to give him a long cool stare from her pale yellow eyes.

chapter seven

The two chairs had already been carried out into the open and were waiting for them. The hermit brought two mugs of tea from a bottle he had been keeping cold in the flow of his new streamlet. He was no longer using the old Indian metate that had held water for the birds and animals. Now there was a big, rather rusty broiler that might once have been used to bake turkeys. The water flowed into it and out again into a dozen little runnels flowing day and night through the vegetable garden and into the little barley field.

Beside one of the runnels two or three of the pagoda lilies were growing.

"I transplanted them a few days ago," said the hermit, following Dave's glance. "I expected the flowers to drop off, but they haven't yet. They may later. And birds! They bathe all over the place now. They feel safer here than by the stream and don't have to keep always on the lookout."

Dave couldn't help saying, "Bet you're glad Grandmother Cat found you."

The hermit didn't say yes or no, for just then there was a scramble of small hoofs and a pony-sized creature appeared, with long ears, a cream-colored muzzle, and a black cross down his mouse-colored back and shoulders.

"Is this the burro?" cried Dave, running over to pat the creature.

"Look out for his heels," warned the hermit. "Neddy's like his master. His temper's not predictable."

While Dave stroked the burro's head and scratched his ears, the hermit went into the cabin and came out with some dry crusts.

As he opened the door Grandmother Cat darted inside, and the hermit waited a minute until she was ready to come out.

"She wants to see if there have been any changes inside as well as out. There's been one big change, thanks to you two, but I don't think she'd notice it. I've tapped

the waterfall with a second pipe which goes into the
cabin to an old sink someone gave me, and then runs
out again over the cabbages. It's very convenient."

Dave blurted, "Who gave you all the pipes and things
and that broiler and sink?"

The hermit glanced at Dave for a moment and he
was sorry he had asked the question.

"That would be telling," the hermit said, smiling.

" 'Them that asks no questions won't be told no lies,' as my grandmother used to say."

"I'm sorry," Dave muttered. "It's none of my business."

"But I will tell you where Neddy came from," the hermit went on, handing Dave the crusts for the burro. "He belonged to Captain John Smith."

Dave looked up in surprise. "But Captain John Smith lived a long time ago. Pocahontas saved him when her father was going to kill him, didn't she?"

"Yes, he's well known in history. They tell about him in all the schoolbooks. I suppose that's why Neddy's prospector picked out the name. It came into his mind and one handle's as good as another when you're looking for a name. He was Captain John Smith and I'm the hermit. They do to answer by."

"But who *was* your Captain John Smith?" Dave persisted, sitting down beside the hermit, who had settled in one of the chairs, first bringing Neddy a washbasin with a few oats in it.

"I can't really feed any of the animals," he said. "I just give them a small treat now and then. You'll see. Neddy will eat the oats and then he'll go, after taking a lick or two of salt from that white salt brick beyond the watering trough. He doesn't really like me. He thinks I separated him from Captain John Smith."

Grandmother Cat jumped onto Dave's narrow lap, and curled herself about as well as she could for a snooze. As for Neddy, he did just what the hermit said he would. He ate the oats, licked the salt, and disappeared down the stairs, head first.

"Who was Captain John Smith?" Dave repeated. He knew that this was a question he might ask and he did want to know. "Was he the man who built the cabin?"

"Good heavens, no!" exclaimed the hermit. "That must have been built when Neddy's great-great-great-great-great-grandfather was a foal. I probably haven't put in enough 'greats' but you get the idea. No, Captain John Smith was an old-time prospector I found back in the hills a way. I say 'old-time' but he was a youngish man himself, though I only saw that later. When I found him he'd broken his leg and had been without food or water two, three days. He had a fever and was unconscious and he might have been a hundred years old to look at him. Neddy was standing right over him, on guard against coyotes, I'd say. He heehawed his head half off when he heard my step. I looked good to Neddy that afternoon."

The hermit stopped talking and seemed to think for a while, remembering the scene. He no longer repeated what he said when he talked with Dave. He'd got used to talking again and seemed to like it, but sometimes he paused to think, as he did now.

Suddenly he went on again.

"I had an awful time getting Captain John Smith aboard that burro. At last he kind of came to and thought I was an Indian and was going to scalp him. He was delirious of course. There've been no Indians hereabouts for fifty years, as you probably know. Neddy saw he didn't take to me and tried to drive me off. But I persevered. In the end I got the captain on Neddy's back, holding him up like a sack half filled with potatoes. The trip back to the cabin was one I wouldn't like to take again.

"And then getting up the steps! I couldn't have managed it if Captain John Smith hadn't come to himself a little by then. He held on to the pack saddle and somehow we all managed. I got his leg into splints with no thanks from him. Whether conscious or unconscious he was cursing me most of the time. I put him on my bed and slept on the floor. He was here for weeks, cursing me, and the food I gave him, and the world in general. Neddy tried to stay in the cabin, but I drove him down into the canyon to forage for himself. Even then, he'd sneak up to see the captain whenever he thought my back was turned."

"I don't think Captain John Smith was a nice man," said Dave.

The hermit laughed.

"He wasn't. And contradict? That's the only way he

53

knew how to talk. I'd say something and no matter what it was, he'd contradict it. I was glad when he was well enough to go. Oh, he wanted to go as much as I wanted to have him. He hobbled down the steps, with me in front ready to catch him if he tripped. Then I helped him down the canyon a way and he tied Neddy to the first sycamore.

" 'You can have him for your pains,' he said. 'What would I want with a burro?' I asked. 'You're lucky to get him,' he said, ugly as ever. 'I could take him with me and sell him if only for dog meat. But he's a good burro. I'll leave him here to pay you.'

"I didn't say anything more and here Neddy has been ever since. His master was going to hitchhike his way to Los Angeles where he had a married sister. He'd had enough of prospecting. It would be something else again next time."

The hermit paused for a little while.

"I respect Neddy," he said. "After he was tied up I walked on with Captain John Smith for another five or ten minutes, about all either of us could stand of the other's society, by then. I figured Neddy thought maybe I killed Captain John Smith, since he never came back. He's a one-man burro and his man was Captain John Smith, the only person, besides you, who's ever been here in my time. Yes, I figure he thought I'd killed Captain John. But he's not quite sure."

Grandmother Cat jumped off Dave's lap and stretched. She was old and thin and Dave's thin legs didn't make much of a snoozing place. When she moved, Dave looked up and his glance traveled down to the far-off valley below them. The only man-made thing he could see was the peak of Mr. Dunhill's big barn beyond the invisible reservoir. Something was fluttering there, and, distant as it was, Dave made out that it was an American flag.

He stared at it.

"That wasn't there when we sat down," he said. "Mr. Dunhill's run it up since I came. Could it mean anything, do you think?"

"Most things mean something," said the hermit comfortably. "The thing is to figure out what it is they mean. And I'll bet you dollars to doughnuts you won't figure this out."

Grandmother Cat was washing herself at the edge of the barley patch, beginning with her gray paws. The hermit looked at her.

"Maybe I'm wrong," he added. "With Grandmother Cat's help you may figure it out. We'll see."

chapter eight

When Daddy was going to give Mother a present he always meant to keep it a secret. But for one reason or another he almost always told her about it days before he intended to. It was a family joke.

On the evening of this particular day when the candles were lighted on the dinner table and grace had been said, Daddy turned to Mother.

"There's a blue roan I've been looking over at Dunhill's for your birthday," he began, and all the children shouted with laughter.

Mother didn't laugh. She just gave Daddy a grateful smile.

"Is he big enough to carry me?" she asked, for she was a tall, broad-shouldered woman, too big for a light horse.

"He's big enough," said Daddy, "and handsome enough and young enough. But he's vicious."

"He won't let anyone come near him?" Mother asked. "He bites and kicks?"

"No," said Daddy, beginning on his dinner. "He lets anyone come right up to him, but when Dunhill got on his back in the ring he began to buck. Gosh, he bucked like an outlaw. You know Dunhill's a good rider. He stuck right to him. Then what does this crazy beast do, but rear? He reared so high he fell over backward. Dunhill slipped out from under, but the creature knocked most of the wind out of himself. He lay still a minute or two before he scrambled to his feet, looking groggy."

"I don't want to have a horse fall over backward when I'm riding," said Mother. "Probably I'd be underneath and a good deal groggier than the horse. Oh, dear! He sounds just right otherwise."

Daddy ate for a little while in silence. "After seeing him put on that performance, I'd say he's a horse I'd never trust, but . . ." He paused while he ate a little more.

"But?" asked Mother eagerly.

57

"Dunhill says to come down Tuesday afternoon. He says by that time that horse will be gentle as a lamb."

"As a ram," said Elizabeth and laughed at her own joke.

"Mother, don't try to ride a crazy horse," said Dave seriously. He knew his mother was willing to try out any horse and it worried him.

"We'll see Tuesday," she said gaily. "We'll all go down and look over my birthday present together. I can hardly wait."

Tuesday afternoon they were all at the ring watching Mr. Dunhill saddle the blue. He was a beautiful horse, big and free-moving. He never flinched as the saddle went on and Mr. Dunhill swung into it. Quietly but with spirit, he walked once around the ring, then trotted, then cantered. His gaits were very fine. Mother was flushed with happiness, holding tight to Daddy's arm.

"Oh, he's just what I've wanted. What a wonderful, wonderful present!"

Dave had walked down to Dunhill's. He liked that better than driving down in the crowded car, and besides he hadn't taken Grandmother Cat exploring for days. She was at the rail now, watching what went on in the ring in her own expressionless way. But later on, when he looked down, after seeing Mother mount and ride off on the new horse, Grandmother Cat was gone.

Dave looked all about him and was just in time to see her easing her way in through the door of the big barn.

"Grandmother Cat!" he called, but she didn't so much as turn her head.

"Mice," thought Dave. "I'll pick her up later." So he waited until Mother had finished her ride in the ring and Daddy had told Mr. Dunhill that he'd take the horse, and Mother had kissed Daddy twice in her excitement, and everyone had piled into the car to drive home.

"Aren't you coming, Dave?" called Daddy, but Dave shook his head and said no, he'd have to find Grandmother Cat first. They'd walk back.

"Oh, come along, Dave," the children shouted. "That old cat can find her way home without your help."

But Dave shook his head again and the car drove off.

Mr. Dunhill had unsaddled the new horse and turned him loose in the corral before he started back into the house with a nod to Dave.

Then he seemed to think of something.

"Like to see if we can rustle up a glass of milk and a couple of doughnuts in the kitchen?" he called back.

"No, thank you," said Dave.

"There's nothing new in the barn that would interest you. You'd better come have the milk and doughnuts," Mr. Dunhill repeated.

But Dave only shook his head again, and Mr. Dunhill went into the house by the back door, looking as if there were something he'd like to say, but didn't know just how to put it. For once, Dave didn't notice anything unusual. His mind was fixed on finding Grandmother Cat.

Dave called her again and then went into the shadowy hay-smelling barn. The hay was piled up in bales, leaving a narrow passage all the way down the center of the barn. Otherwise the bales stretched from wall to wall.

Grandmother Cat did not appear.

Dave walked slowly down the passage, calling to Grandmother as he went. At the very back of the barn he was surprised to see another passage on the left close to the wall. Here Grandmother Cat appeared, tail held high as it always was when she was especially pleased.

The moment their eyes met, Grandmother Cat turned and walked back along this side aisle and disappeared around a corner. Dave followed, and found himself in a small room walled with hay, the top open to the barn

roof. In it the hermit was sitting on a kitchen chair
reading the Bible. On the floor beside him there was a
real mattress made up with sheets and blankets and a
pillow. Beside it stood a covered basket that smelled of
things to eat, and nearby there was an electric lamp.

"Hello, Dave," said the hermit, putting a stalk of hay
to mark his place as he closed his book. "I'm not surprised to see you, but you seem surprised to see me."

Dave sat down cross-legged on the mattress and Grandmother Cat curled up beside him.

"Oh, no, I'm not surprised," he said.

The hermit gave one of his rare laughs.

"I wish you could have seen your face when you came around the corner!" he said. "If you weren't surprised, I'll eat my bear-paw sandals."

Dave grinned.

"What are you doing here?" he asked.

"These are my winter quarters," the hermit said. "I'm only using them now for a night or two. I'll be going home tomorrow. But this is where I come in the fall when my vegetable garden is gone and the snow gets down into the upper canyons. Oh, no. I don't stop being a hermit. Mr. Dunhill and I have an understanding. I spend the winter gentling his stock as I just gentled that horse for your mother. Mostly I work at night. Mrs. Dunhill leaves hot food at sundown at the barn door and baked beans and corn bread and coffee in a Thermos for the next day. Usually I eat them cold, but if I have a mind to, I sneak out up Dry Canyon a little way and heat up whatever I have in a skillet over an open fire. Sometimes I walk up to the cabin to make sure that everything's all right and maybe if the weather's good I stay a day or two."

"But," began Dave, "but I don't understand."

"It's a long story," said the hermit settling back in his chair, "but I'll make it short. I was working here for Mr. Dunhill when I decided to be an all-out hermit. Perhaps that's wrong. I'd already decided to leave Los Angeles and all cities, and get somewhere where I had time to think my own thoughts. I ended up here. It was a great improvement. But even so, there were too many people around. Sometimes I had to talk to buyers or to men wanting to sell or trade a horse. And Mrs. Dunhill is a saint on earth, but she's an awful talker. So I heard a rumor about a ruin on the flats and decided to have a try there. I put on a roof and the windows—you know all about that—and there I stay until cold weather sets in. Then I come here and help about the place like one of those brownies that's useful but never seen. Mrs. Dunhill understands now. I get my keep and often she'll add something else that she knows I could use, especially things of her husband's that aren't worn out. We're the same size and she practically takes the clothes off his back to give to me. Other times she'll put a pot or a pan or canvas or rope by the door. She's one of the friends I told you I had. And he's the other. Sometimes in winter he'll come in to see me for a half hour of talk. I like talk, but only once in a while and with someone I like. He was the one got me those pipes and things to irrigate the flats, and helped me install them, too. But mostly it's our understanding he doesn't come to my place. What they give me isn't charity. I work for it. Mainly in winter, but sometimes at other times, like this, too."

"And that's why the flag was up!" cried Dave. "Mr. Dunhill wanted you to gentle that blue horse for Mother!"

"You've hit the nail on the head," agreed the hermit. "If you live to be as old as Grandmother Cat you may be almost as wise as she is."

Dave grinned and settled down for a talk. But the hermit opened his Bible again and gave the boy a slightly irritable look.

"I've talked enough for a week," he said. "Go away now, like a good boy, and take Grandmother Cat with you. Next time I should be at the cabin, but make sure the flag isn't flying on the barn. Why don't you come about ten days from now? My voice should be rested by then."

chapter nine

Ten days later Dave and Grandmother Cat slipped unnoticed into Dry Canyon and climbed the ridge. Grandmother Cat followed her own invisible footsteps, but Dave carefully chose a new route until they were safely in Fern Canyon, guarded by the dam. The lilies were gone, and the bushes on the slopes were no longer in bloom and the stream ran lower and more quietly, but it was still to Dave the most beautiful place in the world.

That was the day when Grandmother Cat, who as usual was a little in the lead, stopped in her tracks and suddenly flattened to the ground. Dave almost stepped on her before he, too, could stop. Then he stood still, looking on every side to see what had frightened her. He saw soon enough. Slipping off among the bushes, climbing diagonally up the steep slope, moved a great tawny shape, as large as a deer. Once the round head turned and stared at him. He saw the long tail, curling up at the tip.

"Mountain lion!" he thought. And then with relief, "He's not interested in us."

In a few moments the mountain lion was gone like an apparition. Dave breathed more freely, and slowly his heart stopped pounding. Grandmother Cat straightened up from her crouch and moved on, as if she were walking on eggs. Everything was as it had been, yet nothing seemed the same.

The hillsides were more shadowy, the ferns moved mysteriously, the sycamores were like watchers, stiff and uneasy.

Dave was glad when he and Grandmother Cat were safely up the stone steps. There in front of the cabin sat the hermit with an empty chair beside him.

"So you saw my cougar," he said. "She was here on a visit, but didn't stay long."

"How do you know we saw her?" asked Dave. He could never understand how the hermit seemed always to guess what had been happening.

"I use my eyes," said the hermit. "Nothing but the mountain lion could have made Grandmother Cat's hair stand on end, even after she's climbed the steps, and your own hair looks as if it had been standing a little on end, too. Perhaps I only think that. But you both seem extra glad to be here. You needn't be afraid of her. She never disturbs anything in this canyon. Even the deer are safe here. And a lion's distrustful of anything with the human smell. It took me months before I won her confidence."

"You look a little tired, too," said Dave.

The hermit nodded. "Yes," he admitted. "Maybe I am tired. Every time I see that lion, I have to make her understand again that I am really her friend. She thinks so, but she's never quite sure."

There was a clatter on the stairs and Neddy appeared.

"Here's someone else whom the lion has disturbed," said the hermit. "It's all right, Neddy. Wait half a sec. I have some crusts for you."

Neddy ate as usual, suspiciously and half unwillingly.

The hermit brushed the moist crumbs from the palms of his hands on the legs of his pants.

"You've been here with me for three years, Neddy," he said. "And still you hate me. Still you're longing for that no-account master of yours. You're stupid but I have to admit that you're faithful. I think it's about time you had a new master or maybe two. It might start you thinking along other lines."

The hermit regarded the burro for a while as if considering the possibilities of something.

Then he turned to Dave.

"If you'll excuse me a moment, I have a letter to write. I'll ask you to deliver it to Mr. Dunhill. Come on, Grandmother Cat. I might as well invite you. You'll be in like a streak anyway, the moment the door opens."

Dave sat in his chair—it was a comfortable one—looking down the canyon and thinking about the mountain lion.

A few minutes later the hermit and Grandmother Cat joined him. The hermit had a piece of paper in his hand which he folded and handed to Dave. He had brought out with him a length of rope and now fastened it to the halter Neddy still wore.

"Yes, we'll see what a new house and the company of a few horses will do for your disposition," the hermit remarked into the air.

Then he turned to Dave.

"I'm not giving Neddy to you, but to your younger brother and sister who are more his size. Besides, you're riding horses. You've graduated from burros. He's not really mean, I think, except to me. He's let fly with his hind legs at me any number of times. And tried to bite, too. But I think he won't act that way with children. I'm the man who helped tie him up and took Captain John Smith away from him. He can't forget that."

"Suppose Captain John Smith should ever come back?" Dave asked.

"He won't. Anyway, he gave me Neddy, and now I'm giving Neddy to your little brother and sister. If they don't like him they can give him to someone else."

Dave remembered his manners and said, "Jenny and Tom will be terribly excited. It's very good of you, Mr. Hermit."

"I'm only getting rid of a useless mouth," went on the hermit. "He eats oats and crusts that I'd rather give to the deer, let alone the birds."

They sat in the sun talking. When in a talking mood, the hermit liked to hear Dave tell about his family and all the animals that came in and out of the house, or whinnied from the paddock.

"Try putting a ring of moth balls close together around the bushes where the bantams roost," he suggested. "A coyote has a keen nose. He wouldn't like moth balls, I think."

"They come with the full moon," said Dave. "Usually the dogs hear them and rush out through the dog doors, baying. The young dog really roars. Sometimes in the morning they'll have blood on their coats where the coyotes have fought them, but Daddy says those bites are just good-by bites before the coyotes run."

69

"But you do lose bantams?"

"Yes. Sometimes the dogs don't wake up, or wake up too late. I don't think the coyotes make any sound.

The dogs have to get their scent and that depends on the wind."

"It would," agreed the hermit. "You can train a coyote, but he has to trust you first. Mine don't kill anything which they find here on the flats, and they don't do much hunting even in the canyon. After an animal gets to know another animal, he's not likely to kill him. But I'm afraid my coyotes now and then meet with rabbit or quail by the stream with whom they're not acquainted. If they're hungry—and a coyote usually is—they may forget their manners."

Dave laughed with the hermit.

"Try moth balls," the hermit repeated. "I'll be interested to hear if they work."

The hermit was always surprising Dave. Today he brought out two mouth organs and handed one to Dave. Leaning back in his chair he began to play:

"Oh, ye'll take the high road an' I'll take the low road
An' I'll be in Scotland before ye."

Mother often played the guitar or piano while all the family sang, so Dave knew most of the songs that the hermit played and a good many that he didn't.

"You might like this one," he said during a pause. And he taught the hermit the old song about chasing the antelope over the plain, and binding the tiger's cub with a chain.

"I think that's a song your Shakespeare might have sung," said Dave, shy at teaching anything to a grown-up, but the hermit was pleased.

"Now, is it?" he asked. "I like that."

71

And he learned to play the tune on his mouth organ very quickly.

"We'll practice it next time you come," he said.

"Does that mean it's time for us to go now?" Dave asked. He had begun to learn the hermit's ways of doing things.

The hermit nodded and then asked Dave to take the note down to Mr. Dunhill, and to take Neddy, too.

"You can read the letter as you haul Neddy along. If he doesn't haul, get behind him with a stick. That's what he's used to."

As it happened, Neddy made no trouble. He seemed glad to go and now and then reached down his small round muzzle to sniff Grandmother Cat or breathe down Dave's neck.

Dave had plenty of time to read the letter:

"Peter Dunhill, Esq.

"Dear friend," it went, "I hereby give you this burro, Neddy, on the understanding that you will at once give him to Dave to take to his little brother and sister. This way Dave can say he came from you and be telling the truth.

Sincerely yours,
The Hermit

P.S. Truth is important.

H."

chapter ten

Jenny and Tom were delighted with Neddy and so were the rest of the family. If ever a burro was spoiled, that burro was Neddy. The children brought him extra treats until he was as fat as a butterball, but even so, when they took turns riding him with the horses, Neddy kept up with them, walk, trot, or canter. Of course he couldn't walk as fast as a horse. He had a little shuffling trot that he used then, and when they went faster, he broke into a run, his tufted tail flying out behind him.

Dave marveled. The only person in the family Neddy didn't seem fond of was Dave, and only Dave noticed this. When Dave appeared with Grandmother Cat, Neddy didn't come over to the paddock fence to see them but went on doing whatever he was doing before they arrived.

Dave nodded.

"It's all right by us," he told Neddy. "We'd much rather be friends with the hermit than with you. But if you had any brain below those big rabbit ears of yours, you'd know that it was the hermit who saved Captain John Smith and you, too, you silly thing."

Neddy paid no attention to Dave's remarks and Grandmother Cat and Dave went on visiting the horses, ignoring Neddy, which was all right with everybody.

The hermit hadn't set a date for the next visit as he usually did, but Dave decided that ten days would be about right. He marked them off on the calendar in his room.

"Gosh! Can't days go slow?" he asked Grandmother Cat, who raised a drowsy old head from a nap in the middle of his bed, where she seemed to spend more and more time.

On the tenth day it was windy, but Dave decided to go to Fern Canyon anyway. His feet kicked up dust as he walked the skein of dirt roads and paths at the base of the foothills and all the leaves of the bushes were pale with dust, too. It wouldn't rain again for weeks now, maybe months. The pastures were burned to a gold mountain-lion color, except Mr. Dunhill's which were irrigated from the dam at the mouth of Fern Canyon.

Dave caught a glimpse of Mr. Dunhill near the barn and stopped to tell him how well Neddy was making out.

"We might need to borrow him some day to pack more stuff up to the cabin," said Mr. Dunhill. "He took the pipes up. Got them tangled in every bush and tree as we went by. Seemed to do it on purpose. He knew by instinct they were for the hermit. But maybe the hermit won't be wanting anything more."

Dave didn't stop to wonder why not. His mind was on Neddy.

"Neddy's better tempered now," said Dave and looked down to see Grandmother Cat give him her pale owl's stare. "Well, maybe he isn't. He won't speak to Grandmother Cat and me, but he's friendly as can be with all the others."

When they had climbed over the Dry Canyon ridge into their own canyon, everything changed for the better. The hillsides indeed were dry. A shower of small pebbles rattled down wherever Dave stepped, but

75

the leaves were still green, and green plants grew along the shrunken stream bed. The flickering light of running water was still reflected upward on the pale bark of the sycamore trees, as it had been on that first visit so many weeks ago, in the days when they had not known the hermit.

Dave took off his sneakers and waded in the shallows for a while, but the stones were so slippery that he gave it up after two or three splashing falls.

While he put his shoes on again, Grandmother Cat washed her paws.

"It feels lovely to be wet," Dave told her. "Shall I push you in?"

He thought she gave him a look of contempt that set him off laughing.

"I wouldn't dare," he assured her. "You know who you remind me of? Queen Victoria at her golden jubilee. There's a picture of her in the big history book on the bottom bookshelf."

Grandmother Cat obviously didn't know and didn't care to know. Like Queen Victoria, she was not amused.

When they reached the flats, a wind was blowing hard. It was cold and dusty here, too. Grandmother Cat seemed tired. Halfway up the steep uneven stairway of rocks she stopped and gave one of her rusty and infrequent mews.

Dave was a little surprised.

"Want a lift, Grandmother?" he asked and picked her up under one arm. She was so light that she scarcely disturbed his balance. He had not noticed before how very little she weighed.

When they reached the flats, a wind was blowing hard. The hermit and both chairs were indoors.

"Glad to see you," said the hermit when they entered. "Sit you, sit you. It's a good day to stay inside when this kind of wind is blowing."

It wasn't exactly chilly but the hermit had left the last of his breakfast fire burning to embers, and Grandmother Cat, scarcely stopping to rub against the hermit's ankles, went over to the fire and lay down.

"She's tired," said the hermit. "It's probably partly the wind, but Grandmother Cat isn't growing any younger. This is a pretty long walk at her age."

Dave remembered several things at once, the long naps Grandmother Cat was beginning to take on his bed, her asking for help up the steps, and then how light she had felt on his arm.

"You mean she's getting *old*?" he asked, not daring to say more.

"She's always been old since I've known her," said the hermit comfortably. "You call her Grandmother Cat, don't you? She's not sick, if that's what you're afraid of. She doesn't act like a sick animal. It's only that she's getting older. This is a pretty long walk for her now, but she'll still be able to go with you for shorter walks, though probably not as far as Fern Canyon."

"I can carry her most of the way," Dave said anxiously. "It wouldn't be the same without Grandmother Cat."

The hermit was silent for a moment and then he got up slowly and walked over to his little shelf with its two books and took down the old Bible. A large dry leaf marked the place to which he opened the book and began to read slowly,

" 'To every thing there is a season and a time to every purpose under the heaven:

" 'A time to be born, and a time to die; a time to plant, and a time to pluck that which is planted.' "

He was silent for a moment, reading to himself. Then he went on,

" 'A time to get, and a time to lose; a time to keep, and a time to cast away;

" 'A time to rend, and a time to sew; a time to keep silence, and a time to speak.' "

The hermit slowly paused and closed the book and got up and put it back on the shelf.

Dave watched his every movement, feeling solemn and uneasy, unable to say anything.

The hermit came back and sat down again.

He, too, seemed to find it hard to know what words to use.

He cleared his throat. "I guess this is the time to speak, Dave. You might as well learn now that everything in life changes. What's been a fine orange grove becomes a development of little houses, almost alike. You've seen that happen. Even the mountains change a little every year, a new road is cut along their sides, a forest fire kills a grove of big pines in a gully, a landslide carries away a few acres of mountainside. Even the skies change. I suppose every time we see a meteor it leaves the sky just a little changed even if the astronomers can't see it. You change. If you look back, you'll see that most of the things you liked to do when you were Tom's age, you don't care about now. Isn't that true?"

Dumb and numb with a sense of impending doom, Dave nodded, never taking his anxious eyes from the hermit's face.

"Grandmother Cat changes. She can't walk as far as she did a few months ago. Her walks will grow shorter and shorter. After a while she will die, but you must remember that is the way of life. There would be no place for new leaves if the old ones didn't fall. And babies and kittens and puppies and colts, not to speak of fawns and baby foxes!—how could they keep on coming if room wasn't made for them?"

Dave left his chair and stood beside the hermit, putting one hand timidly on his arm.

"You're not going to die, are you?" he asked, almost in a whisper.

The hermit gave Dave a quick hug, over almost as soon as it was begun. "Bless you, no!" he exclaimed. "Not that I know of. All in good time of course, but not yet awhile, I should think. Sit you, Dave, while I tell you what change I was speaking of. You know I wasn't born a hermit."

He laughed and Dave laughed, too, but still uneasily.

"My life happened to take me to cities and after many years I had had my fill of them and the people in them. I still feel that way about cities, but I think since I came here I have learned all that I am likely to learn as a hermit. You and Grandmother Cat have had your share in making me know that I, too, am changing. Why do you suppose I let you see me on the steps the day you first came?"

80

"You had seen us already," said Dave. "You liked us."

"Yes, and why had I paid so much attention to the people I saw riding and walking in the hills? Tell me that, boy. I was getting lonesome. That's what it was, though I didn't admit it even to myself."

"But now you have Grandmother Cat and me—I'll carry her all the way, if she doesn't feel like walking— and you have the Dunhills. You can see them as much as you want to this winter."

"True. But the change in me is deeper than that. Dave, I'm restless. I never thought I would be, but I am. I shan't ever go back to the cities—at least I think I shan't as I now feel—but when we were putting in the pipes Mr. Dunhill talked to me about a friend of his. Seems this fellow raises bees and sells honey. He wants a man who will truck the hives following the nectar— go where the groves are thickest when the oranges and lemons are in bloom; take the bees into the desert when the sage flowers; go up into the mountain mead- ows for the mountain blooms. I'd have a tent and an Australian sheep dog to help guard the hives. And I'd have nothing to do with selling the honey. That's the owner's affair."

"Can you drive a truck?" Dave asked, hoping that he couldn't.

"You ought to see me!" said the hermit, at last smiling. "There aren't many men can drive a truck better than I can."

"But—but it doesn't seem like you," stammered Dave.

"I told you I wasn't born a hermit. I've done a lot of things in my time and I may do a lot more before I die. Probably these years on the Fern Canyon flats will be the best of all, but who knows? I may even come back some day."

"Would you let me know—and Grandmother Cat?" Dave asked eagerly.

"Of course," said the hermit, "but by that time you might be a young man and there'd be no Grandmother Cat. You might not enjoy coming here very much then. It would be like a long-ago story retold when you weren't anxious to hear it. Still, I think we'd always be friends. But I don't really expect to come back. And don't you two visit the flats. A clean break is best. I plan to leave in a few days."

"What will all the animals do?" Dave asked.

"They'll eat up the garden and the deer will eat the barley, and the birds will still come here to drink. They won't remember me long, but maybe for a little while they'll be friendlier to each other. I don't know."

82

"Grandmother Cat and I will remember you as long as we live!" cried Dave, getting up as the hermit rose.

"I believe you will," said the hermit, "and I'll remember you. Your visits were the best thing of the many good things that have happened to me here. For me, too, this will be an especial summer, something to think back on always."

The hermit held out his big bony hand and Dave shook hands with him without speaking. Grandmother Cat had wakened from her nap and now felt the change in the air. She, too, stood up with a little anxious prrp and joined the two in the middle of the low room.

"You'd better carry her down the steps," said the hermit, stooping to run his hand once down Grandmother Cat's rough-haired spine from head to tail tip. "Good-by, Grandmother Cat. In ancient times a man once stood by the bank of a river watching the water flow by. 'Only change never changes,' he said. Remember I told you that, Dave. Now run along and don't look back and don't come back. That's the best way for us all. Good luck always."

"Good luck to you always," Dave tried to say.

The hermit opened the door and Dave went out with Grandmother Cat in his arms. He heard the door

close behind him but he didn't look around. Just for a little while he had difficulty in seeing things, and getting down the steps from the flat was about all he could manage.

Dave's natural obstinacy came back.

"No matter if everything changes as the hermit says," he thought. "I'll remember this summer, every bit of it. And so will Grandmother Cat. That won't change."

And the thought comforted him.

Grandmother Cat was not at all beautiful
Her fur was not like silk, even her purr
Was grating, and her eyes
Were not like amber nor like topazes,
But she was wise.

She was wise, and what was her wisdom?
She knew, just what she wanted to do,
And how to get her own way
Without nonsense or fuss. She obeyed
When she wished to obey.

She was a loner but a heart must love someone,
So she gave her love to the loner Dave,
And he loved Grandmother Cat.
Each loved and was loved, and what
Could be wiser than that?